DILLWEED'S REVENGE

A Deadly Dose of Magic

FLORENCE PARRY HEIDE

with Roxanne Heide Pierce,
David Fisher Parry,
and Jeanne McReynolds Parry

Illustrated by CARSON ELLIS

HARCOURT
Houghton Mifflin Harcourt
Boston New York 2010

Remembering David and Jeanne
with love ~ F.P.H. and R.H.P.

For wonderful Steve Malk ~ C.E.

Dillweed liked to go places.
He liked to have adventures.
He liked to have a good time.

His parents went places.
His parents had adventures.
His parents had a good time.

The parents. Not Dillweed.

One day they set forth on a wonderful adventure.
The parents. Not Dillweed.

Dillweed and his friend, Skorped, stayed home.

Dillweed never went anywhere.
He never had adventures.
He never had a good time.

Umblud and Perfidia were happy that Dillweed's parents had gone away.

When Dillweed's parents were gone,
Umblud made Dillweed do all the work.
The parents were almost always gone.

Dillweed worked very hard.

There was always a new chore for him to do.

HISSS

When Dillweed's parents were gone,
Perfidia made herself the lady of the house.

Dillweed worked very hard.

Dillweed wished he could have adventures.

He wished he could have a good time.

Dillweed thought about Umblud and Perfidia.

Dillweed decided to do something.

Dillweed did something.

Perfidia did not like Skorped.

YAP YAP YAP
YAP YAP
YAP YAP YAP

Perfidia decided to get rid of Skorped.

YAP YAP
YAP YAP
YAP

Umblud made a foolish mistake.

Perfidia made a foolish mistake.

Dillweed and Skorped were happy.

Dillweed's parents returned from their adventure.

Dillweed's parents did not like Skorped.

They decided to get rid of Skorped.

Dillweed and Skorped did not like that.
They wished the parents would go away.

They got their wish.

Dillweed went somewhere.
He had adventures.
He had a good time.

Dillweed and Skorped lived happily ever after.

Dillweed and Skorped, not the parents.

The End

Harcourt is an imprint of Houghton Mifflin
Harcourt Publishing Company.
www.hmhbooks.com

The illustrations in this book were done in ink
and gouache on Bristol board.
The hand-lettering was created by Carson Ellis.

Library of Congress Cataloging-in-Publication Data
Heide, Florence Parry.
Dillweed's revenge / Florence Parry Heide; illustrated by Carson Ellis.
p. cm.
Summary: An adventure-deprived young boy's
neglectful parents and abusive servants receive their just deserts.
ISBN 978-0-15-206394-8 (hardcover: alk. paper)
[1. Revenge—Fiction.] I. Ellis, Carson, 1975- ill. II. Title.
PZ7.H36Di 2010 [E]—dc22 2009027599
Manufactured in Singapore
TWP 10 9 8 7 6 5 4 3 2 1
4500218762